Ultimate Science Lab

EXPERIMENTS with HEAT AND COLD

Anna Claybourne

Gareth Stevens
PUBLISHING

Please visit our website, www.garethstevens.com. For a free color catalog of all our high-quality books, call toll free 1-800-542-2595 or fax 1-877-542-2596.

Cataloging-in-Publication Data

Names: Claybourne, Anna.
Title: Experiments with heat and cold / Anna Claybourne.
Description: New York : Gareth Stevens Publishing, 2019. | Series: Ultimate science lab | Includes glossary and index.
Identifiers: ISBN 9781538235461 (pbk.) | ISBN 9781538235485 (library bound) | ISBN 9781538235478 (6pack)
Subjects: LCSH: Heat--Experiments--Juvenile literature. | Thermodynamics--Juvenile literature.
Classification: LCC QC320.14 C5725 2019 | DDC 536.078--dc23

First Edition

Published in 2019 by
Gareth Stevens Publishing
111 East 14th Street, Suite 349
New York, NY 10003

Copyright © Arcturus Holdings Ltd, 2019

Author: Anna Claybourne
Science consultant: Thomas Canavan
Experiment illustrations: Jessica Secheret
Other illustrations: Richard Watson
Photos: Shutterstock
Design: Supriya Sahai, with Emma Randall
Editor: Joe Fullman, with Julia Adams

Printed in the United States of America

CPSIA compliance information: Batch #CW19GS: For further information contact Gareth Stevens, New York, New York at 1-800-542-2595.

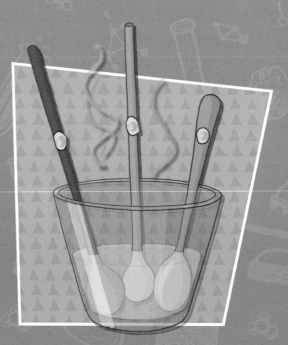

CONTENTS

START EXPERIMENTING!

This book is packed with exciting experiments that use heat and cold to crush objects, make them fly, or are so incredible you won't believe your eyes! But there's nothing magical in these pages—it's all real-life amazing SCIENCE.

BE ECO-FRIENDLY!

First things first. As scientists, we aim to be as environmentally friendly as possible. Experiments require lots of different materials, including plastic ones, so we need to make sure we reuse and recycle as much as we can ...

* Some experiments use plastic straws; rather than buying a large amount, ask in coffee shops or restaurants whether they can spare a few for your experiments.

* Old cereal boxes are great for experiments that use cardboard.

* Save old school worksheets and other paper you no longer need, to reuse for experiments.

WHAT YOU'LL NEED

You can do most of these experiments with everyday items you'll find around the house.

Some useful things to have handy are ...

* Paper and cardboard

* Pens and pencils

* String

* Glue

* Tape

* Straws (plastic ones are best)

* Plates, bowls, jugs, and plastic food containers

* Scissors

* Rubber bands

* Paper cups

* Balloons

STAY SAFE!

Experiments are fun, but some of them can be dangerous if they're not done carefully ... so don't forget these safety tips:

✳ You will need an adult to help with experiments that involve cooking and heating, matches and candles, and sharp cutting tools. Wherever an experiment has something like this in it, you'll see this sign to remind you:

⊙ ASK AN ADULT!

✳ Follow all the instructions carefully to make sure you use all the equipment and materials in a safe way.

✳ If an experiment requires you to stand on a chair, make sure you have someone to assist you. Check that the chair is placed in a stable position and ask the person helping you to hold the chair while you are using it.

✶ Stand back from anything that's moving fast, or that involves eruptions or explosions. And don't throw, shoot, or whirl things around unless you're completely sure there's no one nearby.

And remember...

Always do experiments somewhere that's easy to clean up, like a kitchen or bathroom—NOT on the fancy carpet! And make sure you do clean up after yourself. Some of these experiments are messy!

So, are you ready to see some science? Step this way ...

HOT AND COLD EXPERIMENTS

Heat and cold affect us humans all the time, as we feel them through our skin. In fact, heat and cold have a big effect on everything else, too. Try these experiments to see how!

What is heat?

To us, heat feels pleasantly warm, or painfully scorching, while cold feels cooling, or bitterly sharp. But our experience of heat and cold are caused by just one simple thing—movement.

All matter—the stuff that everything is made of—is made up of tiny atoms, or groups of atoms called molecules. Whether they're in a solid, a liquid, or a gas, they are always moving.

When things get hotter, their atoms and molecules get more energy, and move faster. The hotter things are, the more the molecules move. Heat is simply made of movement. Cold is the opposite—there's less energy, and less movement.

Heat can spread from one thing to another as the movement is passed on. That's why putting your feet on a cozy hot water bottle warms them up!

Hot air, cold air

Try this simple experiment to see what happens to air as it heats up and cools down. You'll need an empty plastic bottle, a balloon, a bowl of water with ice cubes in it, and a bowl of very hot water (ask an adult to get this ready for you).

First, blow up the balloon and let it go down, then stretch it over the top of the bottle. Stand the bottle in the hot water, and hold it there for a few minutes. What happens?

Then move the bottle to the bowl with ice in it, and hold it there. What does the balloon do now?

Changes of state

Heat and cold can also make things change between a solid, a liquid, and a gas. For example, when puddles get really cold they freeze solid. Wet clothes dry quickly in the sun, as the water turns into water vapor, a gas, and floats away. Chocolate melts from a solid to a liquid in your mouth, or when held in your hand.

HOW DOES IT WORK?

The bottle is full of air, which is made of gas. The air's molecules are always zooming around and crashing into each other. When the hot water heats the air, the molecules speed up. They push against each other more, and this makes them spread out and take up more space. So the air expands (gets bigger) and starts to inflate the balloon.

WATCH OUT!

These extreme experiments involve candles, hot water, hot ovens, and freezing ice. Take care when you're experimenting, and have an adult handy to do anything that involves a lot of heat.

HYDROTHERMAL VENT

At the bottom of deep oceans, there are hydrothermal vents, where hot water full of dissolved minerals comes shooting out from under the seabed. This experiment has the same effect—but how?

WHAT YOU'LL NEED:

* A small empty glass bottle, such as a food coloring bottle
* String
* Scissors
* Hot and cold water
* Liquid food coloring
* A large plastic container or bowl
* A pitcher

(!) ASK AN ADULT!

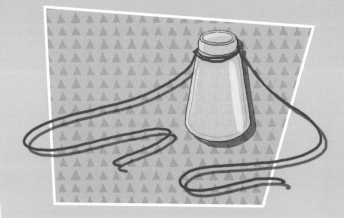

1. Cut a piece of string about 2 feet (50 cm) long. Tie the middle of the string around the neck of the bottle, leaving the two long ends free.

2. Stand your large bowl or container on a table, and use the pitcher to fill it with cold water.

3. Add few drops of food coloring to the small bottle. Then ask an adult to fill it with hot water from the faucet, almost to the brim.

HOW DOES IT WORK?

Like air, water expands and spreads out when it's hotter, becoming less dense. Density means how heavy or light something is for its size. The hot water is lighter than the cold water around it, so it floats up to the top of the bowl, while the colder water sinks. The food coloring lets you see this happening.

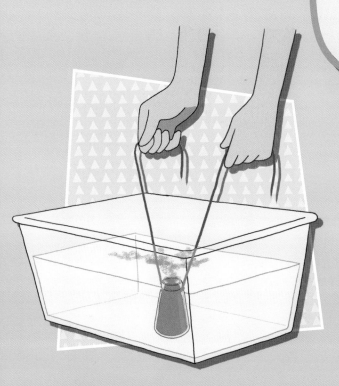

4. Hold the string handles and quickly lower the bottle into the container or bowl of cold water, so that it stands on the bottom. What happens?

SPEED IT UP!

Want your chemical reaction to go faster? Just make it hotter! This simple experiment is an excellent demonstration of how heat speeds up reactions.

WHAT YOU'LL NEED:

* ✱ Two tall, narrow glasses or jars
* ✱ A tray
* ✱ Two small bowls or cups
* ✱ Baking soda (sometimes known as bicarbonate of soda)
* ✱ White vinegar
* ✱ A teaspoon
* ✱ A tablespoon
* ✱ Hot and cold water

⚠ ASK AN ADULT!

1. Stand your two tall glasses on the tray, side by side. Carefully measure three level teaspoons of baking soda into each glass. The amounts must be exactly the same.

Make a "level" spoonful by filling the spoon, then scraping off the top with a knife so that the powder lies flat.

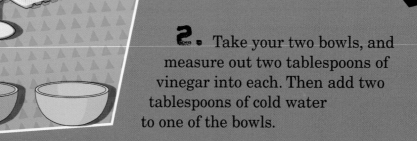

2. Take your two bowls, and measure out two tablespoons of vinegar into each. Then add two tablespoons of cold water to one of the bowls.

3. Ask an adult to add two tablespoons of very hot water to the other bowl (using the hottest water from a faucet, or boiling water from a kettle).

4. Quickly take both the bowls of liquid, and, at the same moment, pour them into the two glasses. Watch them carefully! The tray should catch any mess (hopefully).

HOW DOES IT WORK?

If it works, the reaction in the glass with the hot water will be much faster. This is because of the way heat makes atoms and molecules zoom around more quickly. In the hot water and vinegar mixture, the particles are moving faster, so they crash into and react with the baking soda much more rapidly.

Scientists often add heat to reactions to speed them up.

FROZEN BUBBLES

Bubbles are made of an incredibly thin layer of soapy water. So, before long, they pop! But, using extreme cold, it is possible to freeze a bubble hard. You can do this outdoors on a super-cold day, or with a freezer.

WHAT YOU'LL NEED:

* Bubble mixture and wand
* A very cold day—the temperature must be below −25°F (−5°C)—or a freezer
* A small plate and a straw (if using a freezer)

The outdoor method

1. This is quite simple, but you'll need a really cold day, well below freezing. Take your bubble mixture outside (wrap up warm!), and carefully blow a large bubble. Hold the bubble on the wand, and watch it closely as it starts to freeze.

2. When your bubble has frozen solid, try touching and squeezing it. Does it break, bend, or shatter?

The freezer method

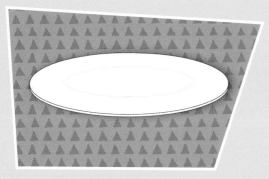

1. First, make some space in your freezer so that your plate can fit inside. Put the plate on a table and pour a drop of bubble mixture onto it.

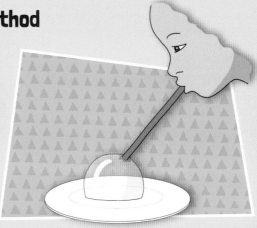

2. Dip your straw in the bubble mixture and blow a bubble into the mixture. The bubble should spread out onto the plate.

3. Quickly but carefully put the plate in the freezer, and gently close the door. Leave it for at least 10 minutes.

You may be able to see patterns of ice crystals that have formed in the bubble.

4. Take the plate out and see if you have a frozen bubble! (It may take a few attempts to get the bubble to freeze without popping.)

HOW DOES IT WORK?
It usually takes water a long time to freeze solid, for example in a pond. But the skin of a bubble is so thin—it only contains a tiny amount of water and soap—that it doesn't take long for the icy cold air to freeze it. The ice forms bit by bit, and spreads across the surface of the bubble.

UNDERWATER CANDLE

Can a candle really burn underwater? Well ... kind of! This experiment uses both heat and cold to give a candle flame an underwater home.

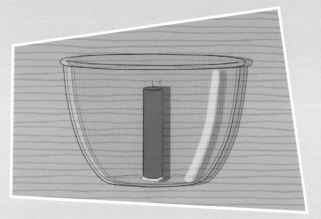

WHAT YOU'LL NEED:

* ✸ A cylinder-shaped pillar candle
* ✸ A large glass or metal bowl that's deeper than the candle
* ✸ Poster putty
* ✸ A pitcher
* ✸ Matches
* ✸ Water

(!) ASK AN ADULT!

1. Roll a ball of poster putty about 1 inch (2.5 cm) across, and stick it to the base of the candle. Press the candle hard into the bottom of the bowl, so that it stands upright and stays in place.

2. Stand the bowl somewhere safe and well away from other objects. Use the pitcher to fill the bowl with cold water, until the water level is about ½ inch (1 cm) below the candle's wick.

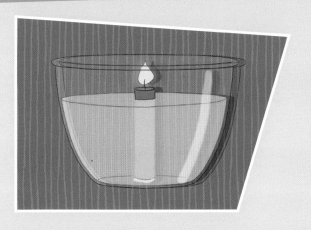

3. Once the water is calm, ask the adult to light the candle. Leave it burning, but make sure there is always an adult in the room to keep an eye on it.

4. The candle will start to burn down. But instead of going out, the flame should get lower and lower, inside a wall of wax that keeps the water out.

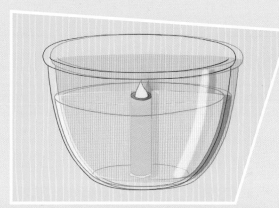

How far below the water level will it go? Can you take a photo from the side, showing the flame rising out of the water?

HOW DOES IT WORK?

When you light a candle, it starts burning down, using up the wax. The heat usually melts some of the wax, too, and it drips down the sides. In the water, the sides of the candle don't melt so much, because the water around them is keeping them cool. Only the wax in the middle burns down, so the flame gets lower and lower—until it's under the water's surface!

PEA AND SPOON RACE

Not an egg and spoon race, but a pea and spoon race! But you don't have to run anywhere—in this experiment, heat is trying to win the race.

WHAT YOU'LL NEED:

* ✹ Three spoons—one wooden, one metal, and one plastic, as similar in size and shape as possible.
* ✹ Three peas, all the same size (not frozen)
* ✹ Soft butter
* ✹ A heatproof glass or coffee mug
* ✹ Very hot water

ⓘ ASK AN ADULT!

1. First, make sure your spoons are clean, dry, and cold, not warm.

If you don't have peas, you can use small, round candies, berries, or beads, or anything of a similar shape.

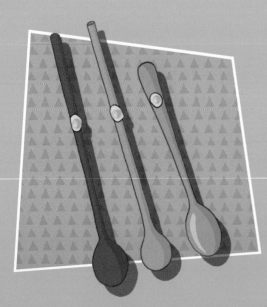

2. Use a dab of butter to stick a pea to each spoon handle. If the spoons are different lengths, line them up, and put the pea the same distance away from the round end on each one, like this.

3. Ask an adult to half-fill the glass with hot water from the faucet. Stand all three spoons in the water, all at the same time. Make them lean away so that their handles are not directly above the water.

4. The race is on! Heat will spread up from the water through the spoon handles. When each spoon handle gets warm, the butter will melt, and the pea will drop off. Which do you think will be first?

HOW DOES IT WORK?

When heat spreads through an object, it's called heat conduction. Some materials are much better at conducting heat than others. For example, metals are good conductors, and heat spreads through them quickly. Wood and plastic don't conduct heat as well.

Heat conduction is one reason we use different materials for different jobs. For example, a pan is made of metal to conduct heat to the food inside, but the handle may be wooden or plastic, so that it doesn't get too hot to touch.

HEATPROOF BALLOON

Can you hold a balloon in a candle flame without it popping? Of course not! Well, actually, you can, with this extreme experiment.

WHAT YOU'LL NEED:

✴ Two balloons
✴ A candle and candle holder
✴ Matches
✴ Water

⚠ ASK AN ADULT!

Do this experiment in the kitchen or bathroom, just in case it goes wrong and you get water everywhere!

1. First, do a test to check that candles really do make balloons pop. Ask an adult to put the candle in its holder in a safe place, and light it. Blow up the first balloon, tie it closed, and ask the adult to hold it over the candle so that it just touches the flame. Pop!

2. Now take the second balloon, and put some cold water inside it. The easiest way to do this is to stretch the opening of the balloon over the end of a faucet. You only need to fill it about a quarter full, then blow it up to full size the normal way.

3. Tie the balloon closed, and dry any water drops off the outside of it. Now ask your adult to carefully hold the balloon over the candle flame, like before.

4. If it works, it should be possible to hold the balloon in the flame for a few seconds, without it popping.

HOW DOES IT WORK?

When the hot flame touches the balloon rubber, it gets so hot that it immediately melts, and the balloon pops. But when there's water in the balloon, the heat from the flame mostly goes into the cold water. It takes a lot of heat energy to warm up water, so it stays cool for a while, and keeps the balloon skin cool, too—even though there's a flame touching it!

MELTING WITHOUT HEAT

Give your friends or family this ice-fishing challenge, and see if they can do it. It seems impossible, until you know the secret!

WHAT YOU'LL NEED:
- ★ A glass
- ★ A tray
- ★ Water
- ★ Ice cubes
- ★ String
- ★ Scissors
- ★ Salt

1. First, fill the glass to the top with cold water, and stand it on the tray (to catch any spills). Put an ice cube in the water.

2. Cut a piece of string about 12 inches (30 cm) long. Now challenge someone to use the string to pick up the ice cube. They can only touch the ice cube with the string, not with their hands, and they can't use a spoon or any other tools.

3. Do they give up? Here's how it's done. Take the salt and sprinkle some onto the ice cube.

4. Carefully lay the string across the top of the salty ice cube, and leave it hanging there for a minute.

5. Now pick up the two ends of the string. The ice cube should be stuck to the string, so you can easily lift it out of the glass.

HOW DOES IT WORK?

Water freezes at a temperature of 32°F (0°C). But salty water has a freezing point that's several degrees lower. So when you add salt to the ice cube, it starts to melt. The string sinks into the melted water. However, melting ice takes heat out of the water, and it gets colder—cold enough to freeze again! The water refreezes around the string, sticking it to the ice

This is why we sometimes put salt on icy roads and sidewalks. As it lowers the melting point of water, it makes the ice melt (as long as the weather's not too cold).

SHRINKING CHIP BAG

Make a perfectly normal potato chip bag into a cute, teeny-weeny chip bag! All it takes is a bit of easy baking.

WHAT YOU'LL NEED:

- ★ An empty potato chip bag (plastic, not foil)
- ★ Baking, greaseproof, or wax paper
- ★ A baking tray
- ★ An oven
- ★ Oven mitts
- ★ A dish towel

⚠ ASK AN ADULT!

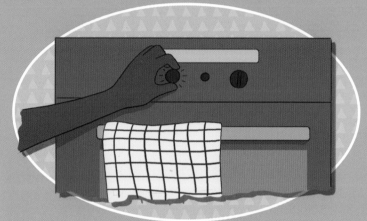

1. First, give your potato chip bag a good wash inside, and dry it completely. Ask an adult to turn the oven on and heat it to about 350°F (180°C).

2. Take a large piece of wax paper and put your bag on it. Smooth the bag flat.

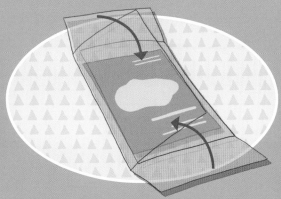

3. Fold the wax paper over the bag on the left- and right-hand sides. Then fold over at the top and bottom to make a simple packet.

HOW DOES IT WORK?

Most things expand or get bigger when they're heated—so what's going on? A potato chip bag is made of a polymer plastic, which is made of chains of molecules. When they are heated, the chains pull together and tighten up, making the packet smaller, thicker, and harder.

4. Turn the packet over and put it on the baking sheet. Ask an adult to put it in the oven. Bake for about 7 minutes. Ask an adult to check it every couple of minutes.

5. When you can see that the bag has shrunk inside the packet, ask the adult to take the baking sheet out of the oven and put it on a heatproof surface. They should then fold up the dish towel and use it to press down on the packet to flatten the chip bag.

6. Once the paper has cooled, unwrap it, and take out your tiny chip bag!

HOT-AIR BALLOON

Hot-air balloons were the first flying machines ever invented. This one isn't big enough to carry a person, but it might carry a tiny paper figure.

WHAT YOU'LL NEED:

* A very large, thin plastic bag— a dry cleaning bag is perfect
* Thin string or sewing thread
* Clear tape
* A small, clean yogurt container to act as a basket
* A blow dryer
* At least one other person to help

⚠ ASK AN ADULT!

1. Lay the plastic bag on the floor with the open end toward you. Cut four pieces of string, each about 8 inches (20 cm) long, and lay them next to the bag.

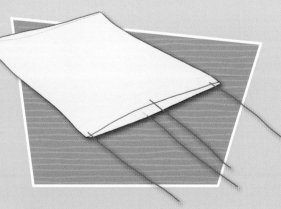

2. Use small pieces of tape to attach the four pieces of string to the open end of the bag, equally spaced around the opening.

3. Tape the other ends of the strings to the sides of the container. You should be able to hold the bag up so that the basket hangs down below it.

Check to see if your bag has any small holes in it. If it does, patch them with tiny pieces of tape.

4. Hold the balloon up while an adult uses a blow dryer to blow hot air into the open end at the bottom. Keep holding the balloon as it fills up with hot air.

5. When the balloon seems to be pulling upward, let it go. If it works, it should fly up into the air, for just a little while—until it cools and comes back down.

HOW DOES IT WORK?

The hot air from the blow dryer is less dense and lighter than the cooler air around the balloon. This makes the balloon lighter than air, so it floats upward. It will work best in cool air—so if you have no luck indoors, you could try this in a garage or yard, if it's colder there.

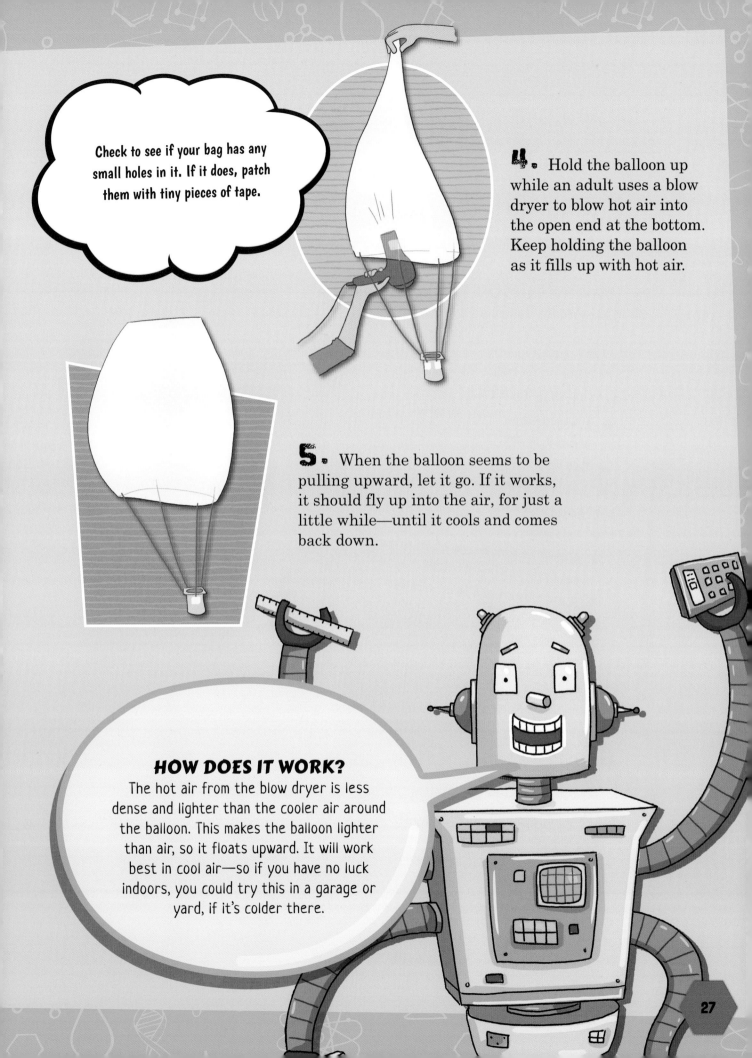

CRUSH THE CAN

Crush a can in a split second using just the power of air pressure! Warning: this experiment is VERY hot, so make sure an adult does it.

WHAT YOU'LL NEED:

* A large container, like a bucket or dishwashing bowl
* Cold water
* Lots of ice cubes
* An empty drink can
* A teaspoon
* A stove—a portable one is best so you can do the experiment outside
* A pair of long metal tongs, such as barbecue tongs
* An oven mitt

⚠ **ASK AN ADULT!**

1. Put the bucket or bowl near the stove. Fill it about two-thirds full with cold water, and add ice cubes to make it even colder.

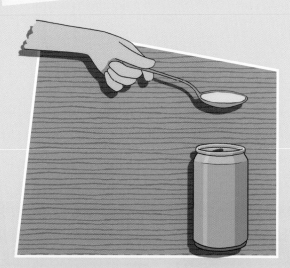

2. Put a teaspoon of water into the can. Ask the adult to switch on the stove. The adult should then wear the oven mitt and hold the can firmly in the tongs.

3. If it's an electric stove, the adult can stand the can directly on the stove once it's red hot. If it's a gas stove, the adult should hold the can over the flame instead.

4. Let the can heat up until the water inside boils, and steam comes out of the hole. Make sure everyone is standing well back!

5. The adult should then use the tongs to turn the can upside down, and quickly plunge it into the icy water. What happens?

The layer of air around Earth is always squeezing and pressing on us, just as it did on the can. We don't feel it because we're used to it, and our bodies are built to resist it.

HOW DOES IT WORK?
When you heat up the can, the air inside it gets very hot. It expands, and most of it gets pushed out of the can. When the can hits the cold water, the air inside suddenly cools and shrinks. But air can't rush back into the can because the water is blocking it. Instead, the low pressure inside the can—and the high pressure of the air and water around the can—squeezes the can and crushes it.

GLOSSARY

atom The smallest possible particle of a chemical element.

conduction The process by which heat is transmitted through an object if there is a difference in temperature.

dissolve To become part of a liquid.

expand To become larger or cover more ground.

hydrothermal Relating to the heated water under Earth's crust.

inflate To expand with air or gas.

mineral A solid, inorganic substance that occurs naturally, often in rocks.

molecule A group of atoms that are bonded together and represent the smallest unit of a chemical.

polymer plastic A type of plastic that is made up of molecules.

pressure A force that is placed on an object.

FURTHER INFORMATION

Books

Andrews, Georgina and Kate Knighton. *100 Science Experiments*. London, UK: Usborne Publishing, 2012.

Homer, Holly. *101 Coolest Simple Science Experiments*. Salem, MA: Page Street Publishing, 2016.

Richards, Jon and Ed Simkins. *Science In Infographics: Forces*. London, UK: Wayland Publishing, 2017.

Shaha, Alom and Emily Robertson. *Mr Shaha's Recipes for Wonder: Adventures in Science Round the Kitchen Table*. London, UK: Scribe UK, 2018.

Winston, Robert. *Science Experiments: Loads Of Explosively Fun Activities You Can Do!* London, UK: DK Publishing, 2011.

Websites

http://www.sciencekids.co.nz/experiments.html
A whole host of experiments that let you explore the world of science.

https://youtu.be/JEWQRJ49CPo
This video will show you how to freeze water with a shake of the wrist!

www.exploratorium.edu/snacks/subject/heat-and-temperature
Discover loads of science experiments that explore heat and cold.

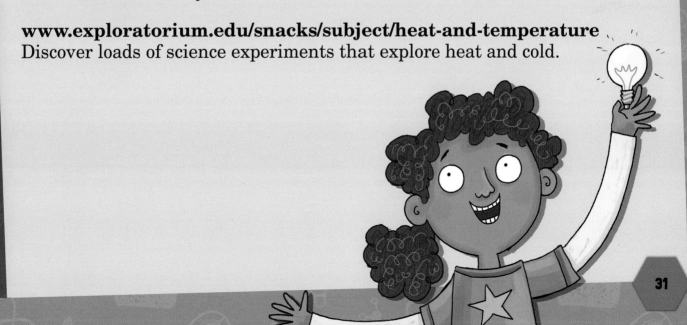

INDEX